William Pricha

A Novella-in-Flash

Diane Simmons

ARROYO SECO PRESS

Logo by Morgan G Robles

Arroyo Seco Press

www.arroyosecopress.org

ISBN: 979-8-9895659-6-2

To Phil, with love

Contents

The Start of It All
1886

William's manager lights a cigar and glowers at him. 'Your attention has obviously been elsewhere of late,' he says. 'I'm disappointed in these sales figures, Prichard.'

William winces. Until recently, Mr Edwards had always addressed him by his Christian name. It's petty of the man. It shouldn't matter now, but it does.

'The company will not tolerate things carrying on in this manner,' Mr Edwards continues. 'Whatever's on your mind needs to be resolved.'

William gets out of his chair, pulls himself up to his full height. 'I understand.'

Once outside the building, he snorts. It's ridiculous—his sales are still the highest in the department. Ideally, he would have liked to stay a little longer with Smiths to assuage his wife's concerns, but he has been left with little choice to resign. It is of no real consequence; he has more than enough capital saved.

After lighting his pipe, he strolls down Cannon Street and joins the hordes heading home over London Bridge. At the railway station, he stops at the W H Smith newspaper stand and assesses the advertisements on display: Beecham's, Abram Lyle & Sons, Twinings and, of course, Harrods. The last few years selling advertising space for Smiths has served him well and he's been good at it; the day he'd struck the deal with Harrods to mark their thirtieth anniversary had been a particularly proud moment. He'd heard no complaints from Mr Edwards *then*.

He buys *The Standard* and walks towards his platform, but just before boarding the train he changes his mind, turns back and leaves the station. With a fractious new baby at home his wife will be hoping for his early return, but him being even more absent is something she will have to get used to.

He hurries through the streets of south London until he reaches Beckett Street. There, he stops outside number three, steps back and admires again the sign he watched the builders erect yesterday: *William Prichard & Co., Manufacturers of Perambulators.* It looks impressive—the deep-blue and white stand out well against the honey-coloured brick. Really, the whole process of setting up the factory has gone better than he expected: it's only been three years since he filed his first patent, a year since he found the premises and set about buying machinery and recruiting staff.

He stays for a few moments, wanders up and down the street assessing his neighbours' buildings. The visit has improved his mood no end. It will be satisfying to contact Mr Edwards in the next few weeks to purchase advertising space for the factory, to see him grovel a little, to be the feted customer, not the disappointing employee.

Trust
1889

It's Sunday afternoon and Eleanor's husband is engrossed in paperwork again. The Lord's Day is a designated day of rest, but William rarely pays heed to that. She takes a cup of tea through to him in his study, hopes the suggestion of a walk in the park with the children will tempt him to stop working. But he declines.

'You should be used to me working long hours,' he says.

'I am. But in the past your hard work was well rewarded. Since you set up the perambulator factory things have been so unsettled. I can't help but worry…'

'You must trust me, my dear—the business will be a success. You said yourself that we have no serious competitors.'

Eleanor sighs. How many times has she regretted complaining to William about the perambulator they'd bought for their first child? If she had not moaned so much, then he would have stayed in his secure occupation, would never have come up with the idea to start his own business. It's all been rather a strain. She's never had to consider money so carefully before; her own family had certainly never worried over it.

William gets up from his desk and kisses her on the top of her head. 'Come and have a look round tomorrow. It will put your mind at rest.'

The next morning, when Eleanor arrives at the factory, William takes her straight to see the elevated runway he's recently had constructed. 'Isn't it marvellous,' he says. 'We can run the prams along the track and inspect the undersides.'

She looks up at the track above her head. Had William told her he'd installed this? She can't remember him doing so, but perhaps she hadn't been listening. He talks a great deal about perambulators, not all of it engrossing.

He takes her on a tour of the rest of the factory: the paint shop, the trimming and upholstery room, the office, the noisy foundry. There seem to be far more workers than there were on her visit last year, and she remarks on this to William.

'We *are* getting fairly crowded,' he says. 'I plan to purchase the building next door. It will be marvellous to be able to expand the paint shop and foundry.' He grabs at her arm. 'Come through and see our latest model—I'm particularly proud of it.'

Eleanor doesn't respond for a moment. He's planning to expand, to take on even more expense? Why has he not mentioned this before? And was he ever intending to tell her about the extra staff he's already employed? She doesn't expect to be consulted, but she should at least be told about such things. She forces her lips into a smile and follows him.

'Isn't it handsome!' he says, wheeling a perambulator out from a long line. 'I've called it The Speedwell.'

She nods. It is handsome—navy blue with an attractive hood and trim and large wheels. She touches the handle, runs her fingers along the smooth wood. Improving the position of the handle had been William's first project when he started designing perambulators. 'May I?' she asks.

'Of course.'

She pushes the carriage across the factory floor, tests the suspension, puts the hood up and down, engages and disengages the brake.

'Are the expansion plans quite settled?' she asks, as she puts it back into its slot. 'Only you have not mentioned it until today.'

He doesn't flinch. 'Almost. I have a meeting with the solicitor next week. I look forward to showing you round when the expansion is finished, my dear.'

She thinks about enquiring about the price he is paying for the new building, but decides against it. There is no doubt that The Speedwell is the best perambulator William has manufactured. Its success is surely guaranteed.

'I look forward to it too,' she says.

Perfectly Put
1891

'You look magnificent, Bertram,' William says when his son walks into the breakfast room.

Bertram bows, removes his cap and examines it. 'That's the school crest,' he says, pointing to the badge on the front. He runs his fingers over the four blue ribbons that criss-cross over the cap. 'I like these too.'

'You're a lucky boy—it's a marvellous school. You must make sure you work hard—I will be relying on your brains when you're old enough to join me in the perambulator factory.'

Bertram giggles and sits down at the table. He displays no signs of nerves for a boy about to start his first day at prep school and tucks into toast and scrambled egg with enthusiasm. He is an impressive child—so clever and self-assured.

As William eats, he allows himself a momentary daydream and imagines an adult Bertram at the helm of the factory. Such a move would enable William to have more free time to pursue other interests such as politics. William Prichard M.P. would sound rather fine, and it would be satisfying to help halt the rise of the blasted Liberals; factory owners like himself should not have to put up with constant government interference. *His* employees are paid well and have excellent working conditions; he hears no complaints.

His younger son calls out to him, and William looks across at him and smiles. Hugh is an exceptionally good-natured child, a pleasure to be around. But he doesn't have Bertram's confidence or academic promise. It's surprising—the operations he endured as a young child meant that he's always received plenty of attention from the family.

'When I'm big, will I work in the factory?' Hugh asks.

'No, no. It will be Bertram. It is always the eldest who follows their father into the family business.'

Hugh screws up his forehead. 'But Clara is the biggest. It should be her.'

Bertram laughs and digs his little brother in the ribs. 'Girls can't do things like that, silly. They need to stay at home to look after the men and children.'

William lifts his son's cap and ruffles his hair. For a seven-year-old, Bertram has such a grasp of things—William really couldn't have put it better himself.

The Brussels International Exhibition
1897

13 May 1897, Brussels

Dearest Eleanor,

I thought Clara and the boys might enjoy this picture postcard showing some of the stuffed animals from the exhibition. Seeing such magnificent creatures has been the highlight for me so far—with the exception of course of seeing our prams in situ & learning they have received the Highest Award! I was so proud I almost telegrammed with the news. Sales will no doubt benefit. I've had stamps made to update our stationery, which I am sure Clara will enjoy using. They will no doubt help make up for her disappointment at not attending the fair—I was correct that it is noisy and busy and not at all a suitable environment for a young lady. There is much amusement to be had here (dancers, fetes, concerts etc), as well as the usual trade exhibits and I find myself so busy I have extended my visit until the 19th.

Fondest love to you, Clara, Bertram & Hugh.

William

Mrs. William Prichard,

14 Manor Street,

Dulwich,

LONDON S.W.

England

7

A Voice
1904

The hall is almost full when Clara gets there and she's forced to sit near the back—all her mother's fault of course for delaying her over a table cloth that had gone missing in the laundry. Why her mother thinks she cares, Clara has no idea.

She flicks through the leaflet she picked up at the door, but is too overheated to concentrate. It would be a relief to remove her coat and hat, but of course even here she can't.

It is days before Clara dare approach her father. The meeting has helped give her courage, but she waits until a large order for the factory and his favourite meal of grilled lamb chops and creamed potatoes finally puts him in a good enough mood.

She takes him cocoa through to his study and waits patiently while he puzzles over a clue in *The Times* crossword. She's practised the speech in her head many times, each time trying to emulate the manner of the speakers at the meeting. Mrs Garrett Fawcett had been particularly composed and methodical in her arguments and Clara needs to be too. Her father will not be swayed by emotion.

Eventually, she is permitted to speak. She tries hard to engage him, but he makes little pretence of even considering her proposal and with a snort returns to his crossword puzzle. Despite her best intentions, she loses her temper.

'But I am the oldest, Father!' she says. 'Why do you favour my brothers over me? I would enjoy being involved with the factory and I am sure my designs would be an asset. Bertram and Hugh certainly show practically no interest.'

He peers over his glasses at her. 'The perambulator factory is not a suitable place for a young lady, Clara. Your mother found occupation as a governess an interesting diversion before we married and I imagine such a position would suit you very well too.'

Clara wants to scream. Her father is too fond of declaring what ladies should and should not experience. 'But you have women working in the factory!'

'Yes. But none of them are my daughter. Your place is here with your mother until you marry.'

With a flick of the hand, he dismisses her, and near to tears, she runs up to her bedroom and tries not to scream. He is such an infuriating man, his arguments nonsensical. It's women who use prams. Most men would not deign to even go near one except to oil the wheels.

She opens her dressing table drawer and removes the leaflet she brought back from the meeting. All the speakers in the hall that evening had been so confident that peaceful means will secure women the vote. She'd left the meeting sure that if men were presented with intelligent argument, they would soon see the error of their ways and success would be guaranteed.

After today, she is not quite so sure.

The Use of Trickery
1905

Hugh is reluctant to agree to Clara's proposal. He is worried, of course, about being dishonest, about their father's reaction when he finds out the truth. But Clara promises to take full responsibility. It will be easy to persuade their father that it was her idea; it is not in Hugh's nature to be deceptive.

Clara hands her brother the pram design. He studies it, then grins at her. It's encouraging to see his reaction. She has at least ten more drawings hidden away, had considered giving him more to look at, but thought better of it. Hugh has not shown the greatest enthusiasm for working in the family business; such sudden productivity might arouse their father's suspicion.

'Just choose your words carefully when you hand it over to him and he'll assume it's your drawing,' she says. 'He'll be so pleased that he won't question it.'

'It is a wonderful design, Clara. I'm sure he'll go ahead with production, but what am I to do then?'

'Once he's committed to it, I'll own up.' She hugs him. 'Try not to worry.'

Hugh's face relaxes a little, but soon he starts to stroke the scars on his top lip. It's what he always does when he's nervous or anxious and Clara wonders again how much the marks affect his confidence. The operations had been years ago and the scars are now quite faint, but it might help if he grew a moustache. She will suggest it.

'It's unfair of Father to not let you be involved in the factory,' he says. 'Why should it matter that you're a girl? You have such original ideas. I can't imagine the frightful drawings I'd produce, though I was rather proud of my recent idea to add an umbrella holder to one of our designs. Father was quite pleased with me for once.'

Clara hugs her brother again, wonders how he can be their father's son. Not that their father is untypical—most men she meets seem to think women belong in the home. It's gratifying that her little brother doesn't agree. He is a sweet boy. Too sweet to do battle with their father every day at work. She would relish the challenge.

'Your umbrella idea is fabulous—and I'm sure you'll come up with lots more. You're a clever boy, Hugh. And you're kind and good. You'll find your way. We both will.'

The Ayah
1906

Clara studies her drawing again. The design of the pram is beautiful: intricate swirly metalwork, long curved handles, two large wheels and two small and an angular hood that's most attractive. It's been exciting to consult the books on India she borrowed from the library and to design something original. Its name, The Ayah, suits it perfectly.

She passes the drawing to her brother, Bertram. He glances at it and laughs. 'You finally got Father to look at your drawings then.'

'I tricked him into thinking it was Hugh's. We both received a stern lecture, but Mother was on my side and Father could hardly refuse after he'd been so impressed. I'm not to be allowed anywhere near the factory though.'

'You need to follow my lead and be firm with Father,' Bertram says. He looks at the design again. 'It's a little fancy, isn't it? Do you think anyone will actually buy it?'

'I think an Indian-themed one might do very well—attract a different type of customer—Indian princes and the like.'

Bertram laughs again. 'Do many Indian princes come to England to buy their prams?'

'I'm sure they do. With their wives. Or perhaps Harrods send their catalogues to India. I'll find out from Father.'

'It's very attractive, Clara, but I'm not sure it will be practical to manufacture. Father needs fewer complicated designs, not more.'

Clara snatches the piece of paper back. Bertram always assumes he knows best about everything, but how can he know best about the pram factory when he rarely goes near the place? He was adamant when he left school that he wished to work in the city, that he had no desire to join the family business. Their father threatened all kinds of punishments, but Bertram stood his ground. As their father's favourite child, he'd got off lightly.

She assesses the drawing again. It's good, but she can't quite believe it's all going to happen. It's just the beginning of her fight though. She would love to be permitted to visit the factory to see it in production, to be given input into the materials and colours, perhaps even to help with the advertisements. But her greatest desire is for her father to agree to a whole series of Indian-themed perambulators. She laughs at her foolishness. To get even this far has taken years.

An Unsure Start
1908

The trimming room is busy—people bustling around, sewing machines whirring, women laughing. It's the last room Agnes goes into. She's found everything in the perambulator factory fascinating so far and has even been introduced to the owner and his son.

Her supervisor, Miss Carter, shows her to her table and introduces her to the other women, then passes Agnes a piece of paper with a design on it. Agnes has never seen anything like it; it looks terrifyingly complicated. She's seen nannies in parks pushing impressive perambulators of course, but in Bermondsey where she lives, most of the babies are carried on their mother's hips or in an ancient rattan carriage. 'Are they all as fancy as this?' she asks.

'Not quite. The Ayah is one of Miss Clara's. There's more than the usual amount of hand finishing and finicky pieces. It's not easy work.'

Agnes looks at the drawing again and feels her palms go sweaty.

'You'll be trained in all aspects of the work we carry out in the trimming room,' Miss Carter says. 'I'll get you some scraps of material so I can take a look at your sewing, see where we are.'

Agnes is worn out by the afternoon. She can't imagine ever being able to master it all. There are people everywhere and there seems to be no end to the perambulators being worked on at the same time, with shelves and shelves of materials to find and put back in the correct place, everyone busy with different jobs. The speed with which some of the women work is alarming, an elderly woman hammering tacks into the perambulator frames, particularly impressive.

It's nearly home time when the owner's son, Mr Hugh, comes into the room. Soon, he and Miss Carter are huddled together in deep discussion. Agnes hears them both laughing and her stomach begins to swirl. Are they laughing at her? At her sewing? She should have stayed at Rawlinson's where she felt safe. The work had been dull but...

She tries to concentrate, but fails and nicks her finger with the scissors. There's an alarming amount of blood. Hiding her hands under the table, she presses her thumb firmly over the cut for a few seconds, but it doesn't work. She is trying to summon up the nerve to reach for an offcut of fabric to stop the flow, when she realises that Mr Hugh is standing next to her. Has he seen? Is he going to tell her off with everyone looking?

'Miss Carter tells me you have a very neat hand, Agnes,' he says. 'Well done. I hope you will be very happy at Prichard's.'

She somehow mumbles her thanks. She can't believe he took the time to speak to her himself, to reassure her. At her last place the owner had rarely left his office.

When he's gone, Miss Carter comes over with a first aid box and hands Agnes a small bandage. 'Wrap it tight round and the bleeding will stop,' she says. 'Don't worry—I used to cut myself all the time when I first started.'

Agnes looks up at Miss Carter's concerned face and smiles. 'Thank you. I'm not worried.'

The Way Forward
1909

Hugh squirms as he watches Albert sweep the factory floor. The old man is pushing the brush so slowly he's never going to finish on time. Albert has been a good employee, but he's too old for the job now. Hugh resolves to talk to his father again about the way forward; he must be persuaded. Things can't carry on as they are for much longer.

The next day, Hugh asks Albert to come into his office. Hugh can barely look as Albert groans and grimaces as he lowers himself onto the chair; he's in an even worse state than Hugh had thought. Hugh decides to come straight to the point.

'It's time you stopped working, Albert. You're seventy-two now. You need to take things easy.'

Albert bows his head, but he doesn't reply. Hugh realises he started the conversation in the wrong place and tries again. 'You have heard about the new old age pension legislation?' he asks.

'I have. He's a good man, Lloyd George. But five shillings a week ain't enough. If you want me gone, sir, I'll have to get meself another job.'

'It's more for a married couple—seven and six, I believe.' William looks at his notebook, checks his calculations again. 'But I agree it's not enough. I've spoken with my father and we have decided to pay you an annuity of eight shillings a week in addition to what the government will give you. So that would be just over fifteen shillings in total.'

Albert shakes his head. 'I can't take no charity, sir.'

'It wouldn't be charity, Albert. Many employers give their staff an annuity. I propose to send young Billy round with the money every Friday.'

Albert shakes his head again. When he eventually speaks, he sounds bewildered. 'Can I ask how long for, sir?'

'We'll pay it until you die, Albert. Be that five, ten, or twenty years.' He smiles at his employee. 'You can rely on it.'

After a great deal more discussion, Albert is eventually persuaded. It's a relief to have the matter settled. Tomorrow, Albert will no doubt thank Hugh's father profusely. But Hugh is sure no specifics will be mentioned, that nothing as vulgar as the exact amount of annuity will actually be talked about.

He's banking on it.

An Outing
1910

Agnes and her friend Lilian walk on to the sands and watch the men paddling in the sea. They've all rolled up their trousers and are splashing each other and larking about. Their employer's son, Mr Hugh, joins them and Agnes is amazed that soon he's laughing and joking along with them all as if there's no difference between him and them. His father, of course, has stayed on the promenade smoking a cigar, his feet firmly contained in his socks and brogues.

Arms linked, the two women carry on along the beach trying to take everything in: the size of the sea, the smells, the screeching of the gulls overhead. It seems unreal. The day out is all thanks to Mr Hugh of course. According to Polly in the office, it was he who suggested that everyone in the factory deserved an outing to celebrate the large Harrods order. When the trip was announced, none of them could believe it at first—not the day out itself, or that it was possible to get on a train at Ealing and travel all the way to Southend. It's all everyone at the factory has talked about for weeks. Most of them have never seen the sea before today, the filthy Thames the nearest they've got to it.

The two friends explore the beach, both women removing their shoes and giggling at the feel of the sand between their toes. They don't stay on the beach for long though. It's only an hour since Mr Hugh bought all the staff toffee apples, but they're soon hungry again and go off to find a bench to eat their lunch.

Agnes has just finished her fish paste sandwiches and is about to eat a plum, when she sees Mr Hugh. He's coming towards them smiling, a cup and saucer in each hand.

'I thought tea might warm you both up,' he says as he hands them the drinks. Lilian gushes her thanks, but Agnes is mute. He stares at her, his face full of concern. 'Are you quite well, Miss Roberts?' he asks. 'You look a little flushed.'

Agnes gabbles something incomprehensible back. No doubt he thinks her a fool, but he politely asks them questions about their plans, tells them he hopes the day will become an annual treat, listens attentively to their answers.

As he walks away, Agnes thinks how kind he's been today. How kind he is every day.

Lilian is silent as they drink their tea. Has she guessed Agnes's feelings? Is it that obvious? Agnes cannot risk people finding out. No doubt the last place she worked at will have her back. *That* factory is run by an elderly man. He has no sons. There, there will be no danger of falling in love with someone outside her class, someone unobtainable.

Black Friday
1910

A man grabs at Clara's breast and she freezes. Her friend Mary shouts at the ruffian and pushes him away, but he laughs and other men and boys join in, jeering and calling them both names. A well-dressed gentleman approaches and Clara is about to thank him for rescuing them when he pinches Mary's bottom. Screaming, Mary kicks him hard in the shins and the effort makes her topple to the ground. Clutching her ankle, she cries out. A nearby policeman laughs. The crowd surge forward and Clara reaches down to rescue her friend.

Both almost in tears, they struggle to a side street and collapse on to the kerb. Clara is comforting Mary when she looks up and sees him. It could hardly be worse timing: Mary is now weeping loudly, both their dresses are torn, their hair in disarray. Their placards are all but destroyed and the messages unreadable, but Clara's father can be in no doubt as to what they've been doing. He scowls at her, his face more angry, more distorted than she's ever seen.

It's the next morning before Clara is summoned to her father's study. She is in no mood to deal with him after the horror of the day before. He starts to lecture her immediately, the content entirely predictable. 'How long have you been involved with these women?' he asks.

She tries to stay calm. 'The government have left women with little choice. Asquith has reneged on all the promises he made and—'

'Nonsense. Women do nothing to further their arguments marching through the streets, chaining themselves to railings, throwing bricks... I cannot believe you have been so foolish. And *you* have nothing to complain of—you have had every opportunity. I have expensively educated you, allowed you to work in the pram factory...'

Clara almost laughs. Allowed? She's twenty-nine-years-old. 'But I am not taken seriously—you seem to consider my designing work to be merely a distraction until I can find a husband.'

'Well, is it not? It's high time you married. Yesterday's display was shameful. I will not have the business's good name besmirched—you will cease working at the factory immediately and stay at home until you can be trusted.'

Clara opens her mouth to protest again; the only shameful thing about yesterday was how disgracefully so many men behaved. But she decides not to argue again. There's no point. Her father has found an excuse to stop her working, to keep her at home. It's what he's always wanted.

Not waiting to be dismissed, she leaves the room, ignores his shouts. He will not win. If he won't let her be part of the family business, she'll have to find another way to use her talents, to have her voice heard.

Prichard v. Maynard & Co. Ltd.
1910

William lingers over his breakfast. He's not slept well. Yesterday had been a most infuriating day, the court judgement a shock.

His wife, Eleanor, gets up from the table and kisses him on the top of the head. 'At least you tried.'

William grunts. He is not used to failing. He'd felt so sure he was doing the right thing in bringing an action against Maynard & Son, had been confident that he would win. He's still not quite sure why he didn't. How is he to secure the future of the factory if he cannot stop other companies stealing his pram designs?

He butters another piece of toast, liberally spreads it with his favourite thick-cut marmalade. He is in no hurry to get to the factory, is not sure how he will face his workers. Perhaps it would be best to take a day off; the three-day court case was exhausting and surely his son could be left in charge for once. 'I think I will go for a walk,' he says, picking up his toast. 'Tell Hugh when he comes down for breakfast that I won't be at the factory today.'

William walks for most of the morning. He heads first to Dulwich Park, then wanders the streets thinking about the factory, about all the work he has put into it. Much of the innovation in British pram design has been his doing and he'd made sure from the off that his work was protected by patents. That had evidently been a waste of time.

Feeling tired, he goes into a tea shop and eats a scone, then a piece of fruit cake. It restores him a little. He used to be able to walk for miles, to work long hours, but now he finds that he often lacks enough energy to do what he wants in the day. Many men his age would pass on the baton to the younger generation. Perhaps he should too. After all, his son had shown better judgement than he had about the court case, had gone up north to visit the Maynard factory to see things for himself and had come home convinced that there had been no patent infringement. Perhaps William should have listened for once.

He leaves the tea shop and carries on walking until he reaches the factory in Bermondsey. There, he walks up and down the street, admires the four buildings he now owns—a huge change from the modest operation he'd started in the 1880s. He does a quick calculation in his head, realises that it's almost twenty-five years since he first went into production. Twenty-five years? Such longevity is a remarkable achievement. He'd done well to save up the money to open the factory, then to make a success of it with little experience. Not many people would have the ability and tenacity to do that and for the most part his judgement has been excellent. So what if he'd made a mistake in bringing the court case? What is one small error in all these years? And who is to say it was an error of judgement anyway? The judge knew nothing about perambulator design. How could he?

Smiling, William pushes open the door to the factory and marches into his office. It's still only two o'clock—there is still time to accomplish much of what needs doing today. And perhaps in an hour or so he will take a short break, allow himself some time to ponder the best way to celebrate the factory's anniversary—to celebrate a quarter of a century of success.

Suffragettes in Trousers
1912

Clara assesses the two men on the stage then whispers to her friend, 'I'm not even sure why they're here.'

'They're part of the movement, Clara! I heard them speak last week—they were very impressive—particularly Matthew Harris.'

Clara's not convinced. Men have no place at women's suffrage meetings—most men she's met just want to take control. And that ridiculous name they call themselves: 'Suffragettes in Trousers' just makes them look foolish. Of course, they've been helpful with the fight at times, particularly with seeing off the rabble during demonstrations and they have easier access to places without causing suspicion. But it's not their battle.

It's Harris who stands up first to speak and he receives a ridiculous amount of applause. There's no doubt he's a good orator and he talks at great length about men's involvement in the movement, about the recent imprisonment of his friend Pethick-Lawrence. Naturally, that had been shocking, but what about all the women who have been imprisoned and forcibly fed?

When the talks are finished, there are the inevitable cups of tea and buns. Clara is left to entertain Harris while his friend is whisked away by the secretary. She prepares herself for a lecture like most of the trouser men seem to do, but he politely asks her questions about herself and seems to listen. Curious to know more about him, she asks how he became so involved in women's suffrage.

'My sister wanted to study at Cambridge,' he says. 'That was the start of it. I was incredulous that they don't award degrees to women. Elizabeth is the one in the family with the brains—I couldn't just stand by and do nothing—women have always supported men in their endeavours. It's time it was reciprocated.' He blushes slightly. 'I do what I can, though I must confess to rather disliking public speaking. I've had something of a stutter since I was a boy. It's rather sapped my confidence at times.'

Clara is silent for a moment. To stand up in front of an audience when he has such problems is impressive. Public speaking is difficult enough under normal circumstances. 'You spoke well,' she says. 'My brother Hugh has similar struggles — not the same affliction, but...' She is unsure whether to carry on. Discussion about Hugh's problems has never been encouraged at home. But surely, Matthew Harris would understand? She decides to tell him more and when she's finished talking, his face screws up with concern.

'I've been seeing this chap in Harley Street who has helped tremendously,' he says. 'I would be happy to talk with your brother...'

Clara nods and thanks him. Her brother would rather like this man. She rather likes this man. Perhaps a meeting could be arranged between him and Hugh when her father is out of the house. 'Would you care to come for tea one afternoon?' she asks.

'I'd very much like that,' he says, smiling. 'And I would welcome the chance to talk further with you too — I feel we have much to discuss.'

She smiles back. 'I feel that we do.'

An Opportunity
1912

The letter is waiting for Agnes when she gets home from the factory. She examines the envelope and her stomach lurches when she sees the postmark. Trying to ignore her mother's stares, she opens it and reads:

William Prichard & Co.,
Manufacturers of Perambulators
HIGHEST AWARD BRUSSELS EXHIBITION 1897

Telephone No. 4980
Telegraphic Address:
"QUADRICYCLES, LONDON"
1,3,5 & 7 Beckett Street,
Bermondsey,
London S.E.

THE PRITCHARD GIG

THE ARGOSY

November 1st 1912

Dear Miss Roberts,

As you know, I was sorry when you left our employ as I believed you had the ability and the disposition to become very useful in my trimming department.

Now Miss Carter has passed from us, I feel you are losing an opportunity. I think you could well earn thirteen or fourteen shillings weekly at once and better than that soon. Will you not consider returning to work here immediately? This really is a very favourable opportunity of taking a very good place for someone as earnest and helpful as I believe you to be.

There is much work to do and you could help to do it if you do not forget how by being away from it all too long.

Yours very truly
William Prichard

Agnes has barely put the letter back in its envelope before her mother starts. 'From Prichard's?' she asks. She puts her sewing down. 'Do they want you back?'

Agnes studies the envelope again, wonders if her mother has steamed it open. She wouldn't be surprised — her mother had been upset when Agnes had left the pram factory and taken a smaller wage elsewhere. After days of nagging, Agnes had confessed all.

She reads the letter out loud and her mother beams when she's finished. 'To think Mr Prichard took the time to write it in his own hand. He must've thought highly of you.'

Her mother's right. He did. And she'd enjoyed working there. But when she'd fallen in love with his son, she'd had no choice but to leave before anyone guessed her feelings.

'You can't miss an opportunity like this, Agnes. You did the right thing going when you did — it's no good getting ideas above your station, but all that silliness must've passed now.'

Agnes studies her mum's hopeful face. She's no doubt thinking what the extra shillings could buy for the family: new boots for Agnes's brothers, better cuts of meat, perhaps even a day at the seaside.

'Yes, Mum,' she says. 'All that silliness has passed.'

A Chance to Thrive
1913

Clara stares at the lists of meals Cook has sent up. She has no interest in whether they have lamb stew on Tuesday or Wednesday, or whether a Battenburg cake will suffice when her mother calls on Friday. She has little interest in any domestic chores. Since her wedding, she's been so busy: there are maids to be trained up, fabrics and wallpaper to choose, tradesmen to engage… It's not how Matthew promised it would be when she agreed to marry him.

It's late afternoon by the time she's finally free to go upstairs to the bedroom she's been using as her studio. She's managed to snatch a couple of hours during the last few weeks to work on her latest fabric design and is quite pleased with it, but the yellow of the daisies is proving tricky and she's behind where she'd hoped to be. The poor light is becoming increasingly frustrating too.

She is mixing paint when Matthew arrives home. It's always wonderful to see him, but she'd imagined she had at least two hours left in which to work.

'I won't disturb you for long, my darling. But I couldn't wait,' he says, taking some pieces of paper out of his briefcase and handing them to her.

'Writing Paper?'

'They're only prototypes—everything can be changed.'

The sheets of paper are handsome, the gold lettering just perfect. She's been meaning to get their personalised stationery done since the wedding. It's kind of him to think of it, but it hardly seems worth all his excitement. She flicks through them, reads, then rereads. She looks up. 'I don't understand—that's not our address—and the name?'

He claps his hands together and laughs. 'I've found a studio for you. It's a short walk away. You needn't take it if it's not perfect—we can find something else. But the light is magnificent and you'll be able to concentrate there.'

'A studio? Oh, Matthew…' She hugs him. 'But the double-barrelled name? Are we both to be known as Mr and Mrs Prichard-Harris? What will your mother say?'

He takes both her hands in his. 'I wanted to show the world that we consider ourselves equal,' he says. 'And that I meant what I said when I proposed.' For a moment he looks concerned. 'Only if you're happy…'

She laughs. 'Of course, I'm happy. It's perfect. Everything is just perfect.'

A Walk in the Park
1913

Agnes is holding a tack between her teeth in a most attractive way; she looks almost serene as she carries out her work. Hugh could gaze at her profile all day. She's a beautiful woman with the most endearing freckles, her auburn hair done up every day neatly in a bun.

Aware that he's staring, he hurries back to his office. Things cannot carry on like this any longer. Does he dare ask if she would accompany him on a walk one Sunday? It would be awkward if she declines and he has no idea if his feelings are reciprocated. She's friendly of course, but she is obliged to be. And then there is his father. Would he object? Hugh suspects not—his father is many things, but he is no snob and he admires Agnes greatly as a worker.

Hugh decides to ask her. He has no choice.

The next Sunday, as arranged, Hugh calls at Agnes's house in Bermondsey. She answers the door, looking charming in her Sunday clothes and immediately introduces him to her family. Her mother invites him to sit down for a cup of tea.

'When we get back, Mum,' Agnes says. 'Tea and cake would be lovely then.'

They walk to Southwark Park. She is easy company and he feels proud to have her beside him. When they reach the boating pond, they find a bench and sit and talk for over an hour—about the factory, about her family, about her fondness for drawing. He feels no hesitation in asking her to go with him to the National Gallery the following Saturday and she enthusiastically agrees.

It begins to get chilly and he reluctantly suggests it's time to leave. As they approach Agnes's house, she laughs. 'I expect there will be a feast waiting. Mum's in a bit of a flap.'

'I wouldn't want to make work. We could easily have gone to a tea shop.'

'She wouldn't be happy with that. She might not totally approve but…'

Hugh stops walking and looks at her. She blushes.

'Forget I spoke,' she says. 'Mum's just a bit set in her ways—she thinks I'm getting above myself with you being who you are.'

Hugh had not expected that. He knows he's not handsome, though his moustache has improved his looks a little. He can imagine a mother being disappointed about that or objecting to some other fault. But to not approve because of his position? He would have thought many mothers might be pleased.

'I wouldn't want our outings to cause upset between you and your mother,' he says.

She meets his eyes and smiles. 'She will just have to get used to the idea.'

He offers her his arm. 'She will.'

No Record
1914

The marriage certificate is blank where Agnes's rank/profession should be. There's no record of her time as a machinist at Rawlinson's or of her promotion to Forewoman at the perambulator factory. It doesn't show how she fought to hide her feelings for the perambulator factory owner's son or her anguish when her future father-in-law insisted she cease working there. It doesn't show either her subsequent worries about cake forks, side plates or her ignorance about how to address a maid. It just shows the evidence of two people who fell in love. Despite it all.

Speaking Out
1914

It's almost six pm, the factory silent. The last of the ghastly accounts are done and Hugh is waiting for his father to return to lock up. When he eventually arrives, he's smiling and full of talk about the Conservative party meeting he's just attended. It's a good time for Hugh to give him the news.

'I'm afraid they didn't want me, Father.'

His father gives him a look Hugh recognises well. 'There must be some mistake.'

'It was foolish of me to try. I knew my speech problems would be an obstacle.'

'I've never heard such nonsense!'

Hugh takes a moment before he replies. Why can his father not accept that Hugh's speech is not always clear to other people? As far as his father is concerned, once Hugh had the operation to correct his cleft palate as a child, that was the end of it. But it wasn't. School proved that often enough.

He tries his best to sound clear, to be firm. 'It could be dangerous. What if my men misunderstood my commands?'

'I'm sure if you had presented yourself in a better way, then there would have been no hesitation on their part. But even so, it's a preposterous decision—the army must be crying out for a boy with your talents—I'll speak to someone.'

Hugh longs to point out that he's not a boy, that he is twenty-eight and a married man. One minute his father is asserting Hugh is fit to lead his men into battle, the next he's treating him like he's a child. Hugh digs his finger nails into his palms. 'No. Don't. The army will be better off without me. And it means I can stay and help you run the factory—you will have more time for your politics then.'

'Politics can wait. I'd rather you did your duty. And I coped well enough before you joined me—designing my own prams, setting up the business with money I'd saved from sheer hard work. I had no one to help out then and I managed to…'

Hugh starts to hum Faure's Pavane in his head. It's a habit he got into as a child, an effective way to block out things he didn't want to hear—especially rants from his father. If he'd been braver he would never have joined the family pram business. But it had been the easy option to start work there after he'd finished school and he'd loved the familiarity of it, the fact that everyone knew him. He'd felt safe, protected even.

At least from the outside world.

The New Hospital for Women
1917

Agnes's mum is mostly quiet as they are shown around the hospital. The place seems wonderful to Agnes and is exactly as her sister-in-law Clara described it: beautiful furniture, welcoming flowery bedspreads, polished wooden floors. There are even paintings on the walls. Some women have visitors and they are sitting by the beds on comfortable-looking chairs, talking and knitting. The atmosphere is one of calm.

When Matron is momentarily called away, Agnes's mum whispers to her. 'It seems clean enough, but why have your confinement here when you've a lovely home like yours?' She looks around, sniffs. 'I expect this place costs a pretty penny.'

Agnes could scream. Her mum is so predictable. She can never resist getting in a dig about money. It's been four years now and sometimes Agnes thinks her mum will never be reconciled to Agnes marrying 'above herself'. Agnes has struggled too with the different ways her husband's family have of doing things, but she's worked hard at adapting. Her mother needs to too, especially considering there's been nothing but acceptance and kindness from Hugh's parents.

'Hugh's been sent all the details,' Agnes says. 'He's happy with everything. He's ever so glad there's doctors around. They did a good job looking after Clara when Emily was born.'

'Men have no place in childbirth — we never called out the doctor unless there was trouble. Mind, we had the bill to worry about...'

Money again. 'The hospital is only staffed by women.'

'But you said there were doctors...'

'The doctors are all women, Mum.'

Her mum scoffs. 'Women can't be doctors!'

Agnes gently corrects her. It seems like she's forever having to explain things nowadays.

35

Matron reappears and shows them to the rooms where the babies are delivered. Agnes recoils a little, but makes herself look round. She's nervous about giving birth, but she's glad it will be here rather than in a cramped, damp house like her mum did. How can anyone not think that this is a better way?

The tour finished, they walk in silence to Regent's Park. When they're nearly there, her mum stops and looks at her, her face creased with obvious concern. 'That woman we saw at the end—the one with the white coat,' she says. 'She must have been one of them women doctors you was talking about. I feel stupid not knowing.'

Agnes looks at her mum properly for the first time that day. There are dark circles under her eyes and she's very pale. No doubt she'd stayed up late trying to fit in what she won't be able to do today because of the hospital visit. There are always customers waiting for their sewing orders, a husband and sons needing three meals a day and the house to be looked after. Her life is one long chore. *She* has no time for daily reading of the newspapers. And unlike Agnes, she doesn't have the benefit of discussion over dinner while someone else serves and washes up.

'Women haven't been able to be doctors for very long, I don't think,' Agnes lies.

She takes her mum's arm and they carry on walking. Agnes asks her advice on as many things as she can think of, offers to show her the pram she's chosen, makes sure her mum knows that she'd like her to visit when the baby is born.

'Did you see the size of them baths?' her mum asks. 'Think how much hot water they'd take to fill!' She smiles at Agnes. 'I reckon a bath would be just lovely afterwards though.'

Agnes smiles back and agrees. It's the nearest her mum will get to showing her approval. But it's enough.

Two Impossible Things
1917

The content of the letters is mostly hideous. They're not the first Clara's received like this—the league opposing women's suffrage seems to delight in such things. She knows she should just ignore them. But what if they are correct and the Bill goes no further?

Her husband pours her a cup of tea, offers her some toast. 'They're just scared—after yesterday's vote there can be no doubt, Clara. A majority of over 380 in our favour—we could never have dreamt of such a thing before the war.'

'But it's still at the committee stage—they have such influential people on their side. If my own brother and father don't think women should be able to vote...'

'Bertram and your father have no influence or power. I beg you to stop reading. It can't fail now.'

She wishes she had his confidence. It's been such a long battle to achieve even these limited voting rights for women. She's sacrificed so much of her time—time she could have spent concentrating on her design business or tending to their daughter. She opens another envelope, reads and rereads its contents. To receive such a thing on the day after the vote... She starts to cry.

'Clara, please...'

She wipes her eyes and laughs. 'Liberty has accepted one of my designs—the poppy one.'

Matthew reaches across the table, takes her hand and kisses it. 'I'm so proud of you! The vote—your design being accepted—this is just the beginning, my love.'

She passes him the letter, watches as he reads it. That the two things she's strived for most of her adult life have come to fruition only a day apart—after all the setbacks, all the years of hard work, is so perfect. She wipes her eyes again. 'It is.'

A Small Price to Pay
1918

The whole family is in the village hall. It couldn't be avoided, but Hugh has no desire to stand by his father's side.

The candidates are called to the stage and even then, Hugh can't fully decide what he wants the outcome to be. If his father were to win the election, then his duties as a Conservative M.P. would keep him busy, and he would have to hand over the control of the factory to Hugh. To be allowed to make decisions without his father's constant critical gaze would be a relief. At the moment, it's an impossible situation. But can Hugh in all conscience wish for that when if his father were to lose, it would almost guarantee a Liberal gain? The Liberals would then no doubt have a large enough majority to form a government and their plans for more social reform could go ahead. They've achieved so much: the introduction of national insurance, old age pensions and school meals for the poor… But it's just a start. There's so much more that needs to be done.

He closes his eyes as the results are announced, feels his mother's hand grip his arm. What is she hoping for? He has no idea. At times, she's seemed to show some understanding of the plight of the working class, has agreed with Hugh's plans to improve conditions for their workers. But mostly, she displays nothing but support for her husband.

When the applause begins, Hugh opens his eyes and looks towards the stage at his father. He is smiling and shaking everyone's hands with gusto. It's an impressive act. Seconds later, the Liberal candidate moves forward to the front of the stage and begins his acceptance speech.

Hugh struggles to hide his smile. His whole body begins to relax as he listens to the winning candidate's plans for the future—for a fairer society.

Hugh's own lack of freedom is a small price to pay.

Nine Minutes Left
1924

William looks at the office clock. Just nine minutes left until the train to Liverpool leaves. Everyone will be there at the station, waiting. William had invented an important business meeting to avoid going, but no one had looked fooled.

Sighing, he relights his pipe. The blasted thing's done nothing but go out all morning. But then nothing's gone right today—his clothes feel all wrong, he cut himself shaving and he noticed earlier he has odd socks on. It all adds to the humiliation.

He leaves his office and wanders round the pram factory, chatting to his workers. As usual, everything appears to be running smoothly and the order book is full, the factory profitable—he has no right to complain.

When he comes across their latest model, The Roxburgh, he stops. It's an interesting thing, the perambulator—a complex piece of machinery, yet his elder son Bertram has never shown much interest in them. And now he's about to leave London and move thousands of miles away to New York to help out in his father-in-law's cardboard box factory. Cardboard boxes? It's beyond William. What challenge can there be in those for a man of Bertram's talents?

Aware that he's still staring at the pram, that he has not moved from the same spot for minutes, he fiddles with the brake, pretends to inspect the paint finish. It's a handsome model and no doubt a pram for twins will be a huge success. Hugh must be given credit for the idea he supposes. He's surprised William at times, but he's not as much of an asset to the business as his brother would have been. It's intolerable that they are to lose Bertram's brains to another family—surely there must be someone else who can help out his father-in-law if the man really is too ill to continue. Bertram is *his* son.

As he walks back to his office, he glances up at the clock on the factory wall. One minute to twelve. The train to Liverpool will have gone.

All hope that Bertram will one day relent is gone.

Another Way
1925

Agnes is walking to the omnibus stop when she sees her old school friend, Arthur. He's in a long line outside the unemployment office. He looks smart in a checked cap and overcoat, but many of the men are scruffy with unpolished boots and patched jackets; some even have their trousers tied up with string. There are two policemen standing nearby. Policemen?

Near to tears, she turns on her heels and rushes round the corner hoping that Arthur hasn't seen her. She has to find an alternative bus route. Going down the high street would be best—it will be a longer walk, but it will be nice to see some of her old haunts again. She's visited her mum today, but nowadays, she rarely comes home to Bermondsey. Her family has got in the habit of visiting her in Dulwich most Sundays— it's good to help her mother out by providing a meal and her brothers look forward to the weekly ride in her husband's car.

She's only been walking for a few moments when she passes Arthur's old house. There are some children playing marbles in the road, just as she and her friends had done as children. They'd been obsessed, out at all hours. But surely, they'd worn coats or at least a warm jumper in December? One boy, she notices, doesn't even have any boots on.

Fretting about Arthur, about the bootless boy, she goes round the corner into the main shopping street and pauses outside the baker's shop. The smell is just wonderful. As children, they'd tortured themselves gawping inside the shop at the currant buns and doughnuts, but with money in short supply most of the time, treats like that had been rare. She can still remember the longing, the pains in her empty stomach. Mouth watering, she goes inside and buys three Chelsea buns to take home. It's all she can do to not shove one in her mouth there and then.

She carries on along the street, looking in shop windows as she goes and is sad to notice that some of the businesses she remembers are no longer there. Before she realises it, she is nearly at the church where she and Hugh married eleven years ago. She grins as she looks up at the building. What a perfect day it had been. She is still smiling at the memory as she walks on, but stops when she spots another queue. This time it is not just men in the long line, but children and women too. No one is talking and many have their heads bowed as they shuffle into the church hall.

She watches for a moment, waits until the last person has gone in, then follows behind. Inside, it's noisy, with rows and rows of people sitting at long tables eating stew and drinking mugs of tea. It's obviously a soup kitchen. Has it always been there? She has no idea.

Stealing away before she is seen, she makes her way to the nearby omnibus stop and is soon back home in the warm. Within minutes of her arrival, her cook serves her luncheon in the dining room. It's her favourite meal of Dover sole and creamed potatoes, daintily served on the china plates she bought from Harrods. She can hardly bear to eat it, but forces it down. Leaving such delicious food will not help Arthur, or any of the other people she saw in Bermondsey today.

She needs to find something that will.

Back Home
1927

'I thought that I would take the boys to London Zoo tomorrow,' Bertram announces to everyone at the table.

His mother shakes her napkin open with a great deal of force and glowers at him. 'Really, Bertram? I hardly think that's appropriate.'

Bertram works hard at not sighing. His mother's reaction is just exasperating. It's been nearly six weeks since his father died. The whole point of delaying coming to England had been so that his sons could see something of London and not be too limited by mourning etiquette. They may as well have visited at the time of the funeral.

'They will be disappointed, Mother,' he says. 'I promised them before we left New York.'

'You should have known better. I'm sure walks in the park will suffice. And there's church on Sunday. The Reverend Jenkins has been a huge comfort to us all.'

Bertram dares not even look at his wife—she'd been hoping to go to Harrods later in the week and he knows there are things on at the theatre that she wants to see. His mother is never going to approve those activities. Really, this whole trip is turning out to be rather dull. He stares at the soup Cook has just brought in and grimaces. Consommé again? They've only been here four days and this is the second time the brown monstrosity has been served up.

'Can something not be done about Cook, Mother?' he asks. 'The boys have hardly eaten since they arrived and yesterday Michael was rather poorly after being given some pink and white cornflour thing.'

'Why on earth would that make the child ill? Do they not have such things in America?'

'Not that I've seen,' he says. 'Ice creams are rather popular—you wouldn't believe the number of flavours—coffee, strawberry—whatever you like really. And you should see the size of the steaks!'

His mother laughs. 'I hardly thing steak is suitable food for a child.'

Aware that she has sidestepped his complaints he gives up. Why she sticks with such an uninspiring cook he has no idea. He's tempted to push his bowl away, to leave the ghastly soup untouched. But he doesn't quite dare. Without even decent meals to look forward to, how on earth are they going to amuse themselves for the next two weeks? Perhaps a trip to the family pram factory might be allowed—it would be better than nothing. He catches his brother's attention and suggests it. Hugh readily agrees and they fix on a date.

'Excellent,' Bertram says. 'I have some suggestions that you may find very interesting. I know I touched on it yesterday when we talked, but business practices in America are so far ahead of us in many ways, I think a longer discussion is needed. I think you will be very interested in their superior method for—'

His sister laughs. 'Oh, goodness, Bertram! Must *everything* be about America?'

Everyone but Bertram and his wife join in the laughter and he forces himself to smile. They really are the limit. He'd been so looking forward to seeing them again, to telling them about America, about all that he's achieved. But no one seems particularly interested. They obviously have no comprehension of how hard it has been for him taking up the reins of his father-in-law's factory and running a business in a foreign country. But he's done it. And he's been bloody good at it. In America people love tales of success, of overcoming obstacles. False modesty is so English though—he'd forgotten that. He'd forgotten a lot of things about England.

He takes a sip of claret. At least his father's cellar is excellent. And he'd enjoyed his clandestine visit to the pub yesterday for a pint of Fuller's. But it's not enough. Perhaps he should disobey his mother and take the children to the zoo as

43

planned? Or even give up the whole thing as a bad job and book an early passage home to New York. The latter certainly seems the most appealing option at the moment. He could always make the excuse that he has urgent business to attend to.

He glances at his mother. Dare he risk annoying her? He refills his wine glass and looks around the large dining room, takes in the impressive collection of oil paintings, the fine Georgian sideboard his father bought for a good price at auction, thinks about the successful pram factory that must be worth a pretty penny. She owns it all.

He finishes the last of the tepid soup, smiles at his mother and proposes a walk to Brockwell Park the next day, suggests Crystal Palace Park for the day after that.

The remaining two weeks of his visit will soon pass.

Liberty
1929

Clara looks up at the outside of the building, admires again the wooden beams. It's still a thrill to visit the new Liberty shop and her daughters never cease to be excited by the fact that the shop was built using timber from old ships. To them all, Liberty's is a magic place.

Today, as it's a special occasion, her mother joins them, still dressed in her mourning black. Clara has no idea why she hasn't reverted to normal attire; it's been over two years since Clara's father died — more than long enough.

The girls take an arm each and lead their grandmother into the building, then up the staircase, peering over the wooden bannisters each time they reach a new floor, excitedly pointing out the exotic goods they can see on the floors below and marvelling at the beauty of the chandelier hanging in the atrium. When they all reach the third floor, they are greeted by the store manager. The display is in a prominent position and more than Clara could have hoped for; the iris print perhaps her favourite of all the things she has ever designed for Liberty. She's come a long way from her first handkerchief.

'Your father would have been very proud. He would have adored all this,' her mother says, stroking the arm of a nearby sofa.

Clara's husband reaches for her hand and squeezes it and she squeezes back. Her mother talks such nonsense. Her parents' house is dotted with Clara's fabrics: cushions everywhere, a chaise longue in her mother's bedroom, curtains in the drawing room, but they were all put there by her mother; none of it was her father's doing.

'You owe this to him of course,' her mother continues.

Clara almost giggles this time at the predictability of the remark. Her mother can see no wrong in her late husband, will not have him criticised for anything, not even when she disagrees—the arguments all those years ago about Clara not being allowed to work in the family business had been proof of that.

'I'm not sure I understand, Mother.'

Her mother inhales. 'You children forget so much. All these designs you do of flowers and plants—it was he who exposed you to all of that. You must remember all those visits to Kew and the nature walks he took you and your brothers on when you were small—even when he could ill afford the time.'

This latest remark is too much. The walks had been for *him*. There had been no dallying to look at wildflowers, no paddling in streams or playing hide and seek, just ghastly endless trudging along canal paths, over fields and up hills. Once she had lain down on the top of a particularly steep hill and pretended to sleep, hoping he would just forget about her and walk on.

But her mother is right in one respect. She does owe him credit. If he hadn't forbidden her from working in the factory, she would never have sought work elsewhere and none of her success with Liberty would have happened. Her life would have been spent in his shadow.

She kisses her mother on the cheek. 'I remember it all.'

A Prudent Decision
1934

New York, 1 March, 1934

Dearest Hugh and Clara,

We were all so sorry here to receive your telegram about Mother. Whilst we of course knew that her health had been a concern for some time, the news still came as a shock. She was a good mother, grandmother and a devoted wife to Father.

You will by now have received my telegram about the funeral. We are so very sorry to not be able to attend, but I know you will both understand. Things are still very difficult here, with businesses failing frequently and profits low for those that have managed to survive. I feel that it would be negligent of me to leave the factory in the hands of Lindy's young nephew for any length of time. The need to be here has been compounded by one of our main competitors in the cardboard box trade shutting its doors last week and it would be prudent for me to be in New York in order to capitalise on the new opportunities this will afford us.

I must admit to feeling rather melancholy and I wonder if I did the right thing in playing down the severity of the situation in America to Mother. I naturally tried to protect her, but perhaps I was wrong to give her the impression that it was because the factory was so busy that I was unable to leave it, whereas in fact the opposite was true. I have been concerned lately that she may have felt I neglected her.

I hesitate to bring the matter up, but please could you send me details of Mother's will as soon as you have had the meeting with the solicitor. I presume that everything has been divided equally between the three of us, but would be grateful to have your confirmation of that.

With my mind on the funeral, I have just dictated a telegram to my secretary with my suggestions for hymns — Mother and I were both blessed with an ear for music and I know she would have approved of my choices. Important to get it right, I think.

Yours,
Bertram

A Matter of Conscience
1934

'Don't be ridiculous, Hugh,' Clara says, pouring her brother another cup of tea. 'The factory was left to you—Mother was quite explicit in her wishes. And Bertram has his father-in-law's business…'

'But Bertram sounds like he is struggling—it would seem fair to divide ownership between the three of us—I'm sure that that's what Father would have wanted.'

'Nonsense. Bertram will have a third of the proceeds of the house sale *and* Mother's capital—you've worked so hard in that factory—and put up with Father. You deserve it.'

Hugh closes his eyes and leans back in the chair. It's been difficult to sleep since he received the latest letter from his brother. Bertram had been so angry, ranting for page after page about him being the elder son, about the unfairness of him not receiving a share of the family business. It's a relief that he's hundreds of miles away in America.

After leaving his sister's house, Hugh heads straight to the pram factory. He switches on all the lights and goes first to his office. A handsome room, it's still very much as it was when his father occupied it. Although his father has been dead for seven years now, the factory had been so much his, that Hugh sometimes expects him to walk in and admonish Hugh over some error or other. He'd been such a strong presence, so sure of himself and that is what confuses Hugh about the inheritance issue. It seems inconceivable that his father didn't have an opinion on who should ultimately own the factory. He wouldn't have left that decision up to his wife. But if that is the case, why did he not express those wishes in his own will?

Hugh sits down at his desk, smokes a cigarette and tries to make sense of it all. But failing to get anywhere, he leaves his office and wanders round the factory. It's blissfully quiet, but rather eerily full of memories—of past employees, of disagreements, of celebrations. He's spent hours and hours in the building, not to mention all the time at home pouring over accounts, fretting about some decision or other. Thirty-three years of commitment. And what has Bertram done in those thirty-three years? Nothing much to help out, that's for certain. Bertram has always done exactly what he wanted—refusing to join the business and then emigrating to America without any thought for anyone. Their father had been incredulous that his favourite son had let him down.

He returns to his desk and looks up at the portrait of his father on the wall. He and Bertram were so alike—and not just in looks. Both hot headed, neither had Hugh's patience. If the two of them had run the factory together, it would never have worked. But their father would not have understood that. Perhaps, even on his deathbed, he hoped that Bertram would relent and come home to take over the factory. Had this hope resulted in their mother being instructed to wait and see what happened—to make a decision on the inheritance based on Bertram's behaviour? It's impossible to know.

Lighting another cigarette, he retrieves Bertram's letter from his jacket pocket and reads it again. His business has obviously suffered greatly and underneath all the bluster, he sounds a worried man. It would only seem right to help in some way. But it will not be a share of the factory. Clara had been correct—Hugh has earned the right to call the factory his.

New Ideas
1936

To Hugh's surprise, his son is at the factory by nine o'clock. He'd imagined Leonard would want to rest on the first day of his university holidays, but is glad to see him and excited about what new business ideas the boy will have learnt on his course. New ideas are what the family business sorely needs. With Hugh's parents now both gone, there is no one left to object to change.

After a tour of the factory, both men retire to Hugh's office.

'If you could give up your desk for the day, I can look over the books,' Leonard says. 'Or I could take them home if you prefer?'

Hugh gets up from his chair. 'No. No. The room's all yours. I'll take the opportunity to help out in the foundry. It will be a treat.'

When it gets to six o'clock, Hugh pops his head round the door. Leonard is still scribbling away. 'Shall we head home? Your mother will be missing you.'

Leonard puts down his pen and beckons to his father to sit down. 'Could we talk now? I think it might help if we discussed my findings while they're still fresh in my mind.'

Hugh agrees and lights a cigarette. He has to admire the boy's enthusiasm. Leonard has been fascinated by the pram factory since he was small. Much more than Hugh had ever been.

'I think you should limit the number of variations of prams,' Leonard says. 'It's not cost efficient as it is. If a customer wants a different finish or wheel size you just accommodate them.' He thrusts a catalogue at Hugh. 'Just look at all the fabric colours—what on earth's *Myrtle Green*?'

'It's a very popular colour! And variety is what our customers like—it's what makes us unique.'

'There's a reason you're unique—it's not a profitable way to run a business. Profits are considerably down and with the additional burden of a percentage being given to Uncle Bertram for the last couple of years...' He shrugs. 'If you had higher profits then you could pay higher wages—you can't afford to lose the workers' loyalty.'

Hugh tenses slightly. He had gone back and forth over what to do to help his brother out. Part ownership of the factory was out of the question, but it had only seemed fair to provide him with a percentage of the profits. He's made a commitment to Bertram—he won't go back on that. And surely, the wages they pay are not far off the mark anyway, especially with the addition of the modern pension scheme he introduced after his father died.

'You need to streamline things, Father. You should consider moving to a production line like Henry Ford's done with cars.'

Hugh almost scoffs but stops himself. Moving away from the coachbuilding method would be a costly undertaking. Leonard can have no idea about that of course. What can he know about anything after one term at university?

'Perhaps. When the time's right,' he says, and immediately, Leonard begins to laugh.

'Did you really just say "when the time's right"? After everything you used to say about Grandfather.'

Hugh can't believe he said it either. It had been his father's stock phrase. He'd been resistant to any new ideas, had held on with a firm grip to his Edwardian ways. Even when he was busy with his beloved politics, he wouldn't relinquish control. When Hugh eventually got his hands on the business, it had been like taking over from a juggler in the middle of his act.

'You *asked* for my advice!' Leonard says.

'I did. I'm sorry.' He laughs. 'I suppose I'm more like my father than I thought.'

'You're nothing like Grandfather. Let's go home, Dad. We can discuss it all again another day.'

'Tomorrow,' Hugh says. 'We'll talk tomorrow.'

In Tandem
1938

Agnes giggles as they race through the park—it really is such fun on the tandem, especially since Hugh bought the new model a few months ago. She'd never got on with the side-by-side one they'd purchased back in 1920—people tended to stare rather. But she enjoys riding the one they have now and today's outing in the sunshine has been particularly pleasant. She cannot remember when they last spent a Saturday afternoon together—Hugh has been far too busy of late.

When they stop for tea in Dulwich Park, she decides now's a good time to bring up the subject. 'I'm finding myself too much on my own, Hugh,' she says. 'The factory takes up a great deal of your time and now that Leonard is more independent…'

His face creases with concern. 'I'm so sorry, my love. I'm afraid it can't be avoided at the moment—I wouldn't if it really weren't necessary, but—'

She touches his hand. 'No, no. I understand the necessity. I was more thinking that *I* need to do something—to have more occupation.'

'But you have the house to run and there is your work at the soup kitchen—I wouldn't want you overdoing it.'

Agnes almost laughs. She has servants to run the house and her work at the soup kitchen in Bermondsey one day a week is hardly arduous. She could fill her time by volunteering there more days, but the real problem is that she misses Hugh when he is out of the house so much. They used to be such a team.

'I thought that perhaps now that your mother and father are no longer with us to object, that I could return to working in the pram factory.'

'The factory? But we already have a Forewoman and Mrs Bancroft has been with us over ten years…'

'No, I didn't mean as a Forewoman. I thought perhaps I could help out in other ways.'

Hugh's face relaxes. 'Oh, good. Did you have something in mind?'

'I've been giving it a great deal of thought and I know that Mrs Bancroft is sometimes overstretched. Perhaps it might help if I were to train the new girls who join us and I'm sure some of the older workers would be glad to learn new skills too.' She laughs. 'Maybe we could even reintroduce more intricate finishes—remember the prams that Clara designed all those years ago...'

Hugh laughs back. 'Those Indian-style prams were very beautiful. And they sold quite well, particularly The Ayah. But I think today's mother wants something a little more modern.' He reaches for Agnes's hand and squeezes it. 'But you may be on to something with regards to training—not everyone comes to us as skilled as you were. And it would be wonderful to have you in the factory again.' He smiles. 'Just like old times.'

Agnes is surprised to realise that she is crying. She'd been horrified all those years ago, when Hugh's father told her it was not appropriate for her to work in the pram factory if she and Hugh were to marry. She'd not felt able to argue. Leaving had upset her so much—she'd loved working there. Until a moment ago, she'd forgotten quite how much.

No Idea
1943

The telegram is waiting for her on the hall table. It's no surprise to see it there – it's a scenario Agnes has imagined often enough. More usually though, she'd pictured herself at home when the telegram boy arrived and him doffing his cap before silently handing her the telegram. At other times, she'd spotted him through the drawing room window before he'd had the chance to ring the bell, and unable to move, she'd let Cook or the maid answer. Occasionally, she'd visualised her husband taking in the telegram and him choosing to read the news of their son's death alone, before coming to find her in the study, the dining room, the garden…

This time, the real time, everything feels less vivid, like she is watching herself from afar. She stares at the telegram, somehow manages to pick it up, to open it. Shaking, she reads, rereads, tries to make sense of the jumble of words before her: 'Leonard Prichard', 'air operations', 'lost his life', 'sympathy'.

She puts the telegram back down on the table and immediately picks it up again. Despite months and months of rehearsing, she has no idea what to do next. Feeling dizzy, she finds her way to the bottom step of the stairs, sits down and puts her head between her knees. But the dizziness doesn't stop. She can't imagine that it ever will.

There Are No Words
1947

Hugh leaves the room. Agnes doesn't blame him. There have been too many discussions, too much indecision. It's exhausting. They've both spent hours trying to come up with the perfect wording for their son's memorial stone and she regrets now being so harsh about some of the messages people sent when Leonard died. So many of them simply said: *There are no words.* She'd wanted to shout at all her friends and relatives to at least try and say something about her darling boy.

It's been over three years since she read any of the cards and letters people sent. She's not sure that dear Hugh ever managed to read any. Perhaps now is the time for her to look properly.

She retrieves the box from under the stairs and is surprised to see it's almost full. There's far more correspondence than she'd remembered. She scans a few, is pleasantly surprised by the contents of some of them, tries not to get upset again by the inadequacy of others. One lovely letter is from Leonard's former housemaster and is full of tales of Leonard's prowess at cricket and how well he'd done academically. She then picks out one from Leonard's friend Thomas from university. He talks about how kind Leonard had been when Thomas was homesick, how he'd helped when Thomas had struggled with his maths.

Next, she lifts out a thick blue envelope. She has no memory of receiving this and recoils a little when she sees it's from Jack Archibald, Leonard's navigator. Scanning through it, she wonders if she has ever read it, guesses she probably stopped as soon as she realised who it was from. It's difficult to think about the men who had been in the aeroplane with Leonard when it was shot down, those who'd survived and been able to carry on with their lives. Of course, she's proud that Leonard was a skilful pilot, that he had been able to hold the aircraft at a height that allowed the others to escape. But she struggles with the unfairness of it all.

Crying, she wipes her eyes, considers stopping reading, but forces herself to carry on. Jack goes into great detail about that final trip, about Leonard's bravery, about how respected and liked Leonard was. He mentions how his wife is to have a baby, how the flight engineer is to be married soon, how they owe all that to Leonard. Jack is such an eloquent writer; his final sentence captures her son perfectly.

She calls for Hugh, tells him that she's ready. He sits down beside her at her desk and kisses her on the cheek. 'We'll fly out to Hanover as soon as the stone is done,' he says.

She nods. Hands trembling, she copies Jack's words into her notebook, inserts their son's name and dates above them:

Leonard Hugh Prichard 17th June 1917 — 4th October 1943
A brave, clever, kind man
He died for us
And lives on in all our hearts

The Right Time
1950

William Prichard & Co.,

Established 1886

Manufacturers of Perambulators

Telephone No. HOP 3451

1, 3, 5 & 7 Beckett Street,

Bermondsey, London S.E.

THE WHITBY

THE WINCHESTER

15 March, 1950

Dear Bertram,

Everyone else has departed the factory for the day and it's blissfully quiet—an ideal moment to thank you again for your publicity ideas and to let you know how things went. I'm sorry to have been so tardy in reporting back.

The event was certainly enjoyable, with everyone from the factory and members of the public seeming to have a good time. The oversized pram that the men built was a particular success and the three ladies from the trimming room dressed as babies were a huge hit, as was the Foreman from the foundry masquerading as their nanny. The press turned up in force and I've enclosed a photo from 'The Bermondsey Advertiser' which you might find amusing. People also seemed to enjoy looking at some of the older prams we retrieved from storage and at the stalls on the history of the factory. The day was an excellent idea. Thank you.

But (and I hate to do a but), there's been very little discernible improvement in pram sales figures as yet. I know you will say to give it longer, but I am not optimistic. England is a different kettle of fish to

America—what works there in terms of advertising may not be quite so successful over here.

I've spent a great deal of time recently analysing where Father and I went wrong with the factory (I know, I know—we have both done many things right too, but I don't think I'm being too harsh on myself—or him). I fully appreciate what Father did was remarkable—his designs, particularly the earlier ones, were impressive and it was no small feat to save up enough capital to start the business and run it successfully for so long. But in his later years his attention wasn't always on it as much as it should have been. After the patent court case, he lost focus a little and then there was of course his blasted politics. Even with his mind often elsewhere he was loathe to hand over more control to me. But his biggest failure I think was not letting our dear sister contribute to the business—just look at the success she's had designing for Liberty's! He was a man of his time, I suppose.

I am not an innovator like you or Father (I know things have not always been easy for you, but I do admire the success you have made of Lindy's family business after all the challenges you faced) & my greatest regret was not acting immediately when Leonard suggested we modernise. I HAD intended to, but it never seemed to be the right time and then, of course, there was the blasted war. And once Leonard died, I just didn't have the heart. With his university education and a keen interest, the dear boy could have been the making of the factory. Without him to carry on the business, I've been wondering if perhaps now is the right time to sell up.

I've spoken with Clara and she's happy for me to do as I think fit. I know it will mean a loss of income for you, but I would appreciate your blessing. I dread it all if I'm honest—I feel awful letting our staff down—some of them have been with us over forty years.

I hope you and Lindy are enjoying your retirement and that you are making the most of the Florida sunshine. The weather is bitter here in London.

Your affectionate brother,
Hugh

Royal Approval
1951

The photograph in the *Evening Standard* shows a typical Royal family pose: The Queen, the princesses Elizabeth and Margaret, The King, The Duke of Edinburgh, Prince Charles and the baby Princess Anne in her pram. They're all standing next to a fountain and even though they're on holiday at Balmoral, their clothes are formal: the Queen has a hat on and poor little Prince Charles looks like he's dressed for church. It's the pram though that stirs Hugh's interest. He examines it closely, then opens the Prichard's catalogue and flicks through it until he gets to The Whitby model. He compares the two pictures. It is one of theirs. Not surprisingly the Royal family has gone for the most expensive version—twenty-one guineas would be nothing to them.

It's an incredible honour to have royalty use one of their prams and Hugh finds his hands are shaking as he looks at the photograph. There will no doubt be greater interest shown in their prams now, with the newspapers and women's magazines discussing the merits of different styles for weeks, perhaps months. The smart set too will be keen to copy the Royals and sales will soar. He can picture the 'By Royal Appointment' on their letterhead; it would look handsome. If his father were still alive, he would have been thrilled.

Hugh puts the newspaper down and lights a cigarette. It's tempting to take the picture through to show the ladies in the office, the workers on the factory floor. They would love it. Many have been with Prichard's for decades, have stayed loyal when they could have left and earned better wages elsewhere.

But he can't show the photograph to them. They'd see it as hope.

Sighing, he stubs out his cigarette. He mustn't put off his announcement any longer. The contract was signed two days ago—there's no excuse to delay further. It's too late to sit around thinking how things could have been different.

He gets up from his desk, but before he goes out to face everyone, he walks round his office examining the scores of photographs on the walls. There are pictures of all manner of prams, half-forgotten staff members bent over their work and years and years of group photographs of their annual outing to the seaside. There's even a few of Hugh's own early pram designs up there—funny-looking things to the modern eye, but they'd been quite successful in their day. He smiles when he reaches the picture of the first company outing to Southend. Goodness, it had taken a lot of persuasion to get his father to agree to *that*. Changing the old man's mind had never been easy, but he'd occasionally managed it when it had really mattered.

Smiling at the memory of his battles, he walks back to the door and looks out through the glass window at his staff hard at work. All of them will be retained by the new owners, but how many will want to travel to Brixton? And Dobson's, with its modern production line, will be a completely alien environment. It's a concern, but at least the agreement to keep them on is in writing and Dobson & Co. can't wriggle out of it. His father would have thought a handshake enough and perhaps Hugh would have done so too at one time, but he's learnt more modern ways of doing things over the years. It's been some small comfort to know that for sixty-five years Prichard & Co. have provided much needed secure employment, that thanks to his actions, the loyal workforce will be protected from losing their livelihoods. He can do no more.

Finally ready, he opens the office door.

Acknowledgements

William Prichard & Co is a work of fiction, but my inspiration for writing the novella-in-flash came from family letters, catalogues and other material that related to the pram factory founded by my husband's great-grandfather in the late nineteenth century. The cover artwork and other illustrations within the novella were sourced from these family archives. I would very much like to thank everyone in the family for providing me with valuable information and anecdotes, particularly my sister-in-law Sarah Traynier, who climbed into her loft several times to retrieve photographs; my sister-in-law Rosie Simmons for her research and enthusiasm and my late father-in-law Tony Simmons who wrote to me many years ago with memories of the factory.

Thanks must also go to the following people: Phil, Heather, Jamie, Mike and Ally for their love and patience; Ingrid Jendrzejewski, Fiona J Mackintosh and Karen Jones for their generous quotes; Jude Higgins, Jeanette Sheppard, Alison Woodhouse, Karen Jones, Damhnait Monaghan and Joanna Campbell for giving up their time to critique the novella, and to John Brantingham, for his support. I would like to give a special mention to Damhnait, whose words, 'I bloody love it', helped me to continue believing in the novella. Huge thanks are also due to Thomas and LeAnne at Arroyo Seco Press for all their hard work and attention to detail.

Previously Published

Grateful acknowledgment is made to the following journals in which these pieces first appeared in an earlier form:

'No Record' (2021) – *National Flash Fiction Day New Zealand* [online] Available: https://nationalflash.org/2021-micro-madness/

'The New Hospital for Women' (2022) – *Sundial Magazine* [online] Available: https://sites.google.com/view/sundial-magazine/flash/the-new-hospital-for-women

Biography

Diane Simmons lives in Bath, UK. She has been widely published in magazines such as *New Flash Fiction Review, Mslexia, Splonk* and *FlashBack Fiction* and placed in numerous flash fiction and short story writing competitions. She is the author of three published novellas-in-flash: *Finding a Way* (Ad Hoc Fiction), *An Inheritance* (V. Press) and *A Tricky Dance* (Alien Buddha). Both *Finding a Way* & *An Inheritance* were shortlisted in the UK Saboteur Awards. She has been a co-director of National Flash Fiction Day (UK) since 2018 and is a former director of Flash Fiction Festivals (UK) and reader for Bath Short Story Award. An editor for FlashFlood, Diane has judged flash fiction contests such as Micro Madness NZ, Flash 500, NFFD Micro Competition and the online Flash Fiction Festival and has co-edited all six Flash Fiction Festival anthologies. You can read more about Diane on her website www.dianesimmons.co.uk and connect with her on X @scooterwriter.

Another masterly novella-in-flash from Diane Simmons, *William Prichard & Co* is a quiet tale of the 65 years of one family's perambulator business. In just 33 short but satisfying episodes, Simmons manages to portray an entire historical saga. By letting us into the inner life of each character while also showing them through the eyes of others, she builds a fully rounded picture of each family member, and, by the time we reach the moving last line, we are sorry to have to let them go. *William Prichard & Co* tells a deceptively simple story that plumbs surprising emotional depths.

—Fiona J Mackintosh, author of *The Yet Unknowing World*

Diane Simmons is such an excellent author of historical fiction. You know you're reading something that has been meticulously researched, but that research never shows up in info-dumps and is instead filtered through the examined lives of the Prichard family. This novella holds up a mirror to society and the changes in attitudes, industrial practices and politics as one family moves through the end of the 19th century into the 20th. There is humour, there is romance, there is emancipation, but most of all, there is an engrossing story of family dynamics that draws the reader in and makes us root for our favourites. This is historical fiction at its best.

—Karen Jones, author of *Burn It All Down*

Diane Simmons has done it again! Back with her latest novella-in-flash, Diane presents us thirty-three glimpses into the lives of three generations connected to a perambulator factory. The novella starts with the establishment of the business in 1886 and traces the family members' highs and lows for the 65-year span of the business, with everything from class, empire, women's suffrage, mass production, and the changing role of women in the workplace swirling around in the background. With the focus on the individual, human stories at the centre of the story, Diane paints a compelling picture of their celebrations and struggles through keen observation and compelling storytelling. *William Prichard & Co* is everything we've come to expect from Diane's writing: well-researched, sharply written, and full of heart.

—Ingrid Jendrzejewski, Co-Director of National Flash Fiction Day

Printed in Great Britain
by Amazon

47192896R00046